the truth about SANTA

Written by: Chelsea Kerr

Illustrated by: Jessica Norman

To my children,
May you always see miracles
and find the truth.

Copyright © 2022 by Chelsea Kerr

First edition August 2022

Book written and designed by Chelsea Kerr
Illustrations by Jessica Norman

ISBN 978-1-5136-9708-6

Only turn the page if you want to know the truth...

As they say- Once, upon a very long time ago, in a place quite far north of here, there lived an old man.

To some he might seem rather unextraordinary, living alone in a small cottage nestled among snow-laden pines, just outside a village in a remote valley. He lived the simple life of a wood carver. Each day much the same, creating useful things people might need- bowls, chairs, benches, and tables.

You could often find him with his back hunched over, working late into the night by the fire. He never seemed to notice the sawdust in his hair, or that his rug was more wood shavings than wool.

But if you were to look
a little closer, very close in fact,
you may find, hidden among the
odds and ends of unused and
long forgotten scraps, a
beautifully carved and
painted wooden doll,

or a miniature pony so detailed in its design you
might expect it to gallop right out of your hands.

4

I'm sure by now you are wondering why these beautiful treasures seem to be forgotten among the waste and the piles of everyday household items.

You see, the woodcarver wasn't always alone. As a young man, he married his heart's true love and the next winter they were blessed with a beautiful baby girl.

Now, if this story was a fairytale the story would end here with a happily ever after, but you turned the page, so you want the truth. And sometimes, in truth, there is sadness.

Shortly after the birth of their daughter the village was swept with a terrible sickness, and though he did everything in his power, the man lost his beloved wife and daughter.

The next year as the time approached for what would have been his daughters first birthday, he found himself carving a beautiful wooden doll, but the grief over all he had lost overcame him and he placed the doll on a shelf and forgot...

until the next winter...

... and the next, until many years had passed,

each with a beautiful wooden toy in memory of his daughter.

Usually, in any good story about ordinary people, there must be a catalyst- that is, a person or event so great it creates a change, making the ordinary... extraordinary.

In our story this happened one day as the old woodcarver was making his deliveries around the village. He noticed a young brother and sister traveling home from school when all of a sudden, the little girl tripped and toppled right into a muddy, mushy puddle of muck, instantly bursting into tears.

Now, some brothers I know might have poked fun or laughed at a sister in such dire circumstances, but as the man watched, something amazing happened. The brother kindly helped his sister out of the puddle and sat her on the stoop of a nearby shop. He carefully removed a handkerchief from his back pocket and gently wiped her tear-streaked face, hands and knees. He then carefully took her hand and led her home.

The woodcarver returned to his home, so touched by this ordinary but extraordinary act of kindness. When he opened the door to his cottage his eyes fell on the small wooden pony laying among the shavings- and an idea struck.

He hurried around the cottage collecting the pony and the wooden doll, and quickly made his way back to the village.

Night had fallen by the time he crept quietly to the home of the little boy and girl.

In the morning when the children left for school, on the stoop they found a beautifully carved wooden pony and doll.

From then on, as the woodcarver travelled through the village, he watched...

Each time he witnessed small acts of kindness, somehow, as if by magic, a small wooden carving would appear on the doorstep of the child who had performed it. Sometimes he would observe a father out of work, or a mother struggling to feed her children. They would soon find a wooden bowl filled with nuts, fruit, and bread.

For many years the town-folk were delighted and mystified by the random appearance of these gifts, never knowing where they came from.

Over time the children came up with their own stories of a magical elf who delivered gifts in the night to girls and boys who had done good deeds.

Now, as I said in the beginning, this all happened a very, very long time ago, and you may have guessed by now who this old man was. You might also be wondering how one old man lived for so long and how he could possibly know about, and travel to, every good girl and boy....

Are you ready for the truth?

He didn't.

After many years of quietly bringing joy to the children of his village, the woodcarver passed away. He was very old you see, and he was just an ordinary man. There was no magic that could keep him alive for hundreds of years, and no army of elves helping him make millions of toys...

however...

When the people of the village learned of the woodcarver's passing, they sent a young man to his cottage to clean out his home and appropriate his belongings. It just happened that this young man was once a little boy, a boy who helped his sister, and discovered a magical wooden pony on his doorstep.

The young man entered the woodcarver's cottage and tears came to his eyes as he looked upon the shelves overflowing with small wooden toys of all shapes and sizes.

The young man lovingly packed the toys into wooden crates and returned to the village. He shared the secret with his young wife who, after sharing her lunch, had found an ornate dollhouse.

He also spoke to a friend who had once received a set of wooden blocks after helping a widow whose laundry had blown off the line.

Soon, many of those who had been children at the beginning of the magical gifts knew of the kindness and generosity of the old woodcarver.

And then, something miraculous happened-
each of those who had received of the old man's
kindness, started watching... and they too noticed
small and simple acts of kindness. They observed
the struggle and hardship of those around them-
and they all started performing small miracles
for others.

They began **S**erving **A**nother's **N**eed
Truly **A**nonymous.
And thus, **SANTA** was born.

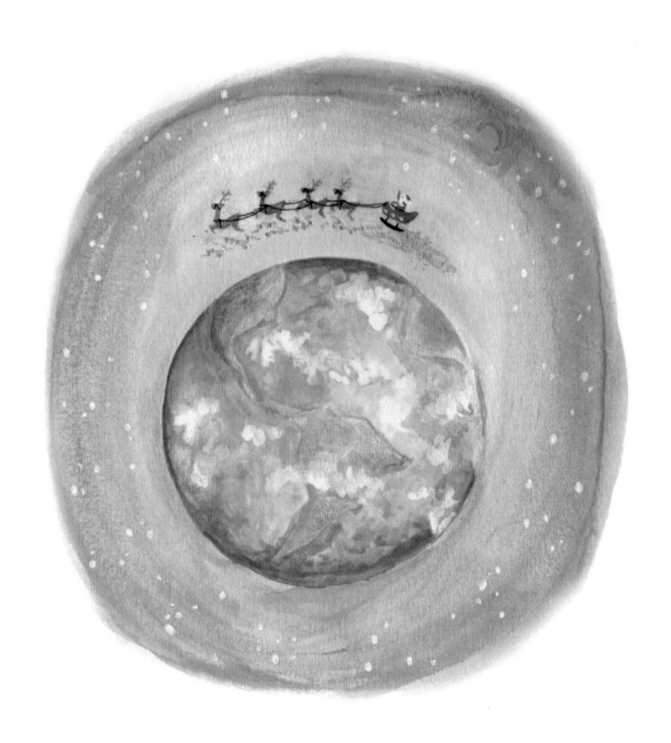

Time passed, some villagers moved away, and the magic began to spread. The keepers of SANTA passed down the legacy of the old woodcarver, and you know how stories spread, they grow and change and sometimes by the end it is very hard to distinguish the truth from the legend.

So... now you know the truth.

SANTA is real.

SANTA is the magic of Christmas and the true spirit of giving.

SANTA exists deep in the hearts of those who selflessly give of their time and resources.

SANTA is found in the delight and wonder of a child on Christmas morning.

SANTA is sharing the love of our Savior with those around us.

SANTA exists in Love, Kindness, and Charity.

Is it not our very belief that gives him his identity?

Now you know...

Now you believe...

Now YOU are SANTA.

34

A note from the author...

Several years ago a friend was looking for a way to
talk to her growing kids about Santa, my own children
were getting close to the same age. I went to bed
that night with many thoughts, and when I woke,
I started writing.. and *The Truth About SANTA*
unfolded.

My family and I have been blessed to
experience many SANTA moments over the
years. The goodness of people helping people is an
amazing force and a legacy I hope my own children
carry on. May you always see miracles and continue
your search for the truth.

~Chelsea Kerr

About the illustrator...

Jessica is a Utah native. She lives in Cache
Valley but loves to travel. This is her first
time illustrating a book, and she hopes you
like her work! She was fortunate to grow
up in an artistic family who instilled a love
of art, and looks forward to whatever
projects the future brings.

Made in the USA
Coppell, TX
30 November 2022

87460425R00024